For Simon
A.B.

For Kate, Marcus and Alice
A.R.

Written by Alan Brown
Illustrated by Adrian Reynolds
British Library Cataloguing in Publication Data
A catalogue record of this book is available from the British Library

Text copyright © Alan Brown 1998
Illustrations copyright © Adrian Reynolds 1998

The right of Alan Brown and Adrian Reynolds to be identified
as the author and illustrator of the Work has been asserted by them in
accordance with the Copyright, Designs and Patents Act 1988.

Published 1998 by Hodder Children's Books,
a division of Hodder Headline Limited
338 Euston Road London NW1 3BH

10 9 8 7 6 5 4 3 2

ISBN 0 340 70961 8 (PB)

Printed in Hong Kong

Humbugs

Written by **Alan Brown**

Illustrated by **Adrian Reynolds**

Hodder
Children's
Books

A division of Hodder Headline plc

In spring the pale sun warms the rich earth. Birds sing and make their nests. Foxes, badgers and rabbits dig burrows for their babies. The buds on the trees open out into fresh green leaves.

In the garden Dad digs and rakes and sows his vegetables. He's looking forward to eating tasty new potatoes, fresh carrots and runner beans. "Vegetables are useful," he says happily.

Simon wants to be a gardener too.
He wants to sow seeds that will grow into flowers.

"I'd like some pretty flowers for the house," Mum agrees.
"But these are for the humbugs," says Simon.
"I don't know about humbugs," Dad says,
"but the garden is full of vegetables.
There's no room for flowers."

Simon searches in the garden and finds spaces
for his flowers that Dad hasn't seen.

Against the rickety fence
he sows Snapdragons.

In the rocky soil next to the shed he sows Evening Primrose.

At the edge of the path where Dad walks between his vegetables, Simon sows Forget-me-nots.

He covers the seeds with soil and waters them
with his own little watering-can.
Diggory Dog wants to dig them up again.
Simon gives him a bone and he buries
it in the middle of the potatoes.

The days get longer and warmer.
The vegetables and the flowers
push green shoots up through
the soil.

Dad sees the flower seedlings.
"What's this?" he says in
surprise. "These are not
cabbages. These are not peas."
"They are my flowers,"
says Simon. "Please don't
pull them up."
"They don't look very useful,"
grumps Dad, but he does not
pull them up.

Every day the vegetables and the flowers grow bigger. They reach up green fingers towards the hot summer sun. The flowers open.

The tall Snapdragons against the rickety fence dangle red bells. The Evening Primroses next to the shed unfold yellow cups, and the Forget-me-nots that creep along the edge of the path look up with blue eyes. The garden is bright with colour.

"Can I cut some of your flowers to take into the house?" asks Mum. "Please leave them for the humbugs," Simon begs.

Simon lies on the path with Diggory Dog and watches his flowers. A humbug hums round the Forget-me-nots. Bzzzz! Bzzzz! It lands on a blue flower and crawls inside to take the sweet nectar. Then it hums away to the hive in the garden next door.

In the hive the humbug hums and
dances with the other humbugs.

Bzzzz! Bzzzz!

It turns this way and that.

Bzzzz! Bzzzz!

The humbug is telling about Simon's
flowers and all that sweet nectar.
There is a great humming.

Lots of humbugs come to Simon's
flowers. They go to every blossom.
They go to the red Snapdragons
against the rickety fence. They
go to the yellow Evening
Primroses next to the shed.
They go to the blue
Forget-me-nots along
the edge of the path.

They crawl inside every red bell, yellow cup and blue eye, and take the sweet nectar. Then they hum back to the hive next door. All the hot sunny summer the humbugs hum to and fro. They love Simon's flowers. Diggory Dog barks at the humbugs, but they take no notice of him.

Simon and Mum go to see the hive.
Mr Beamish next door shows them the honeycombs
where the humbugs store the sweet nectar.

When Simon comes home he is carrying a golden jar. It looks full of sunshine. Mum brings in some of Simon's flowers. She has Snapdragons from against the fence. She has Evening Primroses from next to the shed, and Forget-me-nots from along the edge of the path.

Mum puts the flowers in a vase on the table while Dad spreads toast with sweet honey from the jar.

"The humbugs made the honey," says Simon,
"with nectar from my flowers."
"Mmmm," says Dad with his mouth full.
"Your flowers are useful after all."
"And pretty," says Mum.
"Pretty useful," says Simon. "Can I have
some honey, please?"
Diggory Dog digs up his bone
and brings it in for tea.

Yummy!